Frisbee Goes To The Beach

By Diana P. Woltereck

Illustrations by Paul Treadway

To Alex & Henry
Happy reading
Diana P. Woltereck
2023

To all the gray squirrels in our yard that bring me so much pleasure. To Jim, you are my rock. To Ruby, I will always love you.
- D.P.W. -

To my wife, Janet, my entire family and dear friends for all the love and support they continue to offer.
- P.T. -

ISBN: 978-0-9967453-1-4

Library of Congress Control Number: 2016901547

Printed in the United States of American

∞ This paper meets the requirements of ANSI/NISO Z39.48-1992 (Permanence of Paper)

My name is Frisbee and I am an Eastern Gray squirrel. I live in Aunt Dizzle's back yard.

Don't get me wrong, I love the people that raised me. They saved my life and raised me to be a happy and healthy squirrel. I live in their backyard. But I want to find my squirrel relatives.

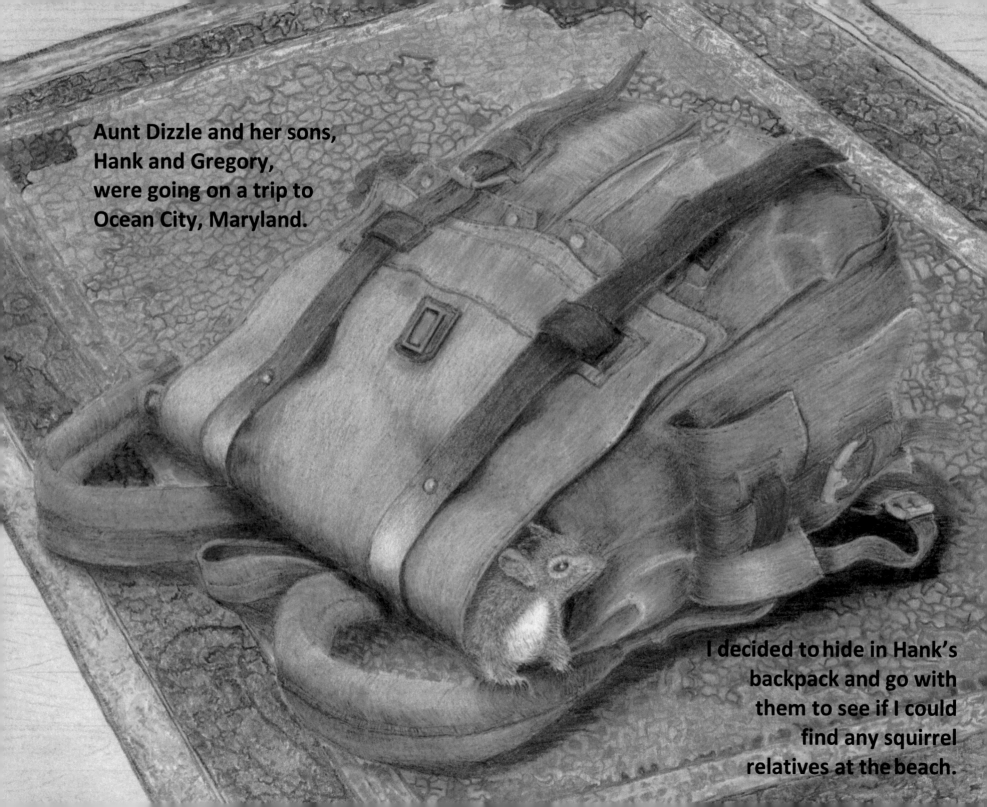

Aunt Dizzle and her sons, Hank and Gregory, were going on a trip to Ocean City, Maryland.

I decided to hide in Hank's backpack and go with them to see if I could find any squirrel relatives at the beach.

We all piled into their
yellow car and off we went.

As we drove along, I decided to hop out of the backpack and jump up on the back seat. The boys were so surprised to see me, but really happy I had joined them.

We travelled for a very long time and drove over this really, really big bridge.

When we finally arrived at the beach, I ran off in search of any squirrels living in the area.

On my way, I came face to face with a really big dog that started barking when I tried to talk to him.

Then he started to chase me. I ran as fast as I could down the beach and hid under the boardwalk.

While I was hiding, I looked over and saw this big bird. I asked him what kind of bird he was. He said he was a Great Blue Heron and lived at the beach all year long. I asked him if he knew of any squirrels that lived around the beach. He told me he knew of several who lived by the bay. So off I went in search of them.

Before I knew it, I ran into a whole family of black squirrels.

They didn't look exactly like me, but I discovered we belonged to the same squirrel family; we are just different colors.

They told me that beach life wasn't too bad; they often come down to the dunes to scamper and play. Although they eat the same foods that I do, sometimes it is hard to find nuts and seeds at the beach. So, they have to bury them just like I do to save for a rainy day.

I am a happy squirrel; on my first vacation I met some of my cousins. As the sun began to set over the bay, I realized I needed to get back to Aunt Dizzle and the boys because we would be going home soon. I thanked my cousins for a fun afternoon and hoped that we would meet again sometime.

Back home, I realized how lucky I was. I have a great human family; live in a really tall maple tree in the backyard and have an awesome house to live in which Uncle Jim built for me. Isn't it cool? In the backyard I am safe and sound. I can sit on my porch and gaze out over my wonderful home.

I spend most of my day, dreaming of my next adventure.
Maybe someday I will find more relatives, but for now
my life couldn't be any better.

Diana P. Woltereck was born in Baltimore, MD in 1948 and was graduated from The Johns Hopkins University in 1989 with masters in Administrative Management. She is also a nurse by training and spent the better part of the last 35 years serving patients and clients in the greater Baltimore area. Her love of squirrels began in 1975 when the family dog rescued three baby squirrels. Over the years Ms. Woltereck rehabilitated many abandoned baby squirrels which lead to her love of these curious, little animals. Ms. Woltereck lives in Parkton, Maryland with her husband Jim Ralls. This is her second children's book in the Frisbee's Adventures series.

Paul Treadway was born in Baltimore, MD in 1949. He is a self-taught, wildlife portraiture artist and drawing has been his passion since early childhood. He considers himself an absolute realist with great attention to detail. Mr. Treadway's primary medium is black and white graphite pencil and a blend of color and pastel pencil. Mr. Treadway currently lives in Millsboro, Delaware, although he and his wife Janet enjoy spending time in their home town of Baltimore, Maryland with family and friends. The Eastern shores of both Maryland and Delaware, with the abundance of wildlife and shoreline, have been an inspiration for many of his drawings.